VOICES
OF a
SANDHiLLS
BABY BOOMER

BY:

BiLL LiNDAU

Azalea Art Press
Southern Pines, North Carolina

ISBN: 978-0-9899961-0-5

Cover Photograph:
John Roger Palmour

DeDicaTion

To the late William Edwin ("Bill Sr.") Lindau
and Mary Elizabeth ("Betsy") Sanders Lindau,
my father and mother, whom I wouldn't have
traded for anything in the world;

To Sara Lindau, my big sister, a say-anything
lady who can be brutally honest with you one
minute and make you laugh until you cry the next;

To a dear departed friend, whom I still miss after
twenty years. She took a genuine interest in me and
my works. She is the inspiration for three poems
appearing in this book;

To my aunt, Sally S. Blankenship and her husband,
George, their five children, their grandchildren and
their great-grandchildren;

And to the many friends, educators and pets who
have made life such a treat!

contents

PReFaCe

It is an honor to tell you some things about my longtime friend and former colleague, Bill Lindau, and to introduce you to this anthology.

Before Bill and I ever met, I was familiar with book reviews he wrote under a pseudonym for *The Pinehurst Outlook* in the 1970s. A few years later, he joined my staff as a part-time sports reporter and photographer and as sports editor of *The Moore County News* and *The Citizen News-Record*. For eleven years, Bill was sports editor of the *Richmond County Daily Journal* of Rockingham. He now works in retail sales and does freelance reporting and photography for several publications.

I found out recently that Bill is more multi-talented than I ever imagined. He is something of a Renaissance man. I have read his poems and essays and have been impressed with the depth of feeling Bill displays.

He has had short stories published. He also sings, plays piano, acts and paints. Bill loves reading and discovering unusual old words and phrases that he might use someday in conversation or writing. He is a movie aficionado and a lover of the arts in general. Bill is a character who loves a good story, joke or pun—or crafting any of these.

Bill is a proud American who loves his home state of North Carolina and living in the Sandhills. He is inspired by nature and his surroundings. He cherishes and never forgets his friends, whether he just met them or has known them since childhood. I am amazed at the number of his friends. This guy is genuine and down-to-earth and usually wears an impish grin that makes you wonder what he's up to.

His writings stem from a creative spirit and a warm, compassionate, romantic heart. In this book, Bill shares a bit of himself and his talents. I know you will enjoy and admire his offerings as much as I have.

Greg McNair

Greg McNair is a retired publisher and editor and is a former owner of Western World, a community newspaper in Bandon, Oregon. He is a native of Rockingham, North Carolina.

iNTRODUCTiON

"Let's take a breath, jump over the side."
- *Coldplay*

This quote from this famous British rock band's hit, "What If" best sums up my decision to put together a collection of my most contemporary writings.

This anthology consists of short memoirs, poetry, song lyrics, a science-fiction novella and the first short story I ever published. Also included are a few poems submitted at the time of this writing. You can read many of them on Facebook.

I don't remember when I learned to read. As the son and brother of three avid bookworms and writers, I can't remember ever *not* reading. From that day I have read voraciously, starting with all the comic books I could get my hands on—especially the old *Classics Illustrated* comics—and including my parents' vast collection of time-honored works, including the *Harvard Classics* series and the hardbound volumes of *American Heritage* and the old *Horizon* magazines. You name it, I read it.

Then one day in my early childhood I thought, "Wouldn't it be great if people enjoyed the things I'd write the same way I enjoyed Shakespeare, Mark Twain and Homer?" As a fat kid with chronic asthma—always the last pick in the fifth-grade recess games—I did not give a hoot for sports, but I loved my rainy-day afternoons diving into all my parents' books!

In high school I started a novel based on my friends and our typical teenage antics. I showed it chapter by chapter to my classmates. What a mistake! Some of them weren't exactly jumping for joy, and so I told them that I burned it—which I did, after two months of working on the novel in secret. Then I got frustrated and got rid of it. And so, despite that early failed attempt, the publication of this book is the fulfillment of a lifelong dream.

I have had a good writing career as a reporter, book critic, sports editor and copy editor for the former *Citizen News-Record* of Aberdeen, the *Richmond County Daily Journal* and other small, local newspapers. I have also had six short stories and numerous poems and short memoirs published before this, in college and "little" literary magazines, and many contributions in *The Fayetteville Observer's Saturday Extra* edition.

In one more bit of horn tooting, I'll always remember the first time I had my fiction published. "The Girl with the Dirty Face" appeared in the spring 1982 edition of *Colonnades* magazine, out of Elon College. They paid their contributors in complimentary copies. Mine must have gotten lost in the mail, for I did not find out about it until someone said they saw my story mentioned in then-publisher Sam Ragan's column in *The Pilot*, the local newspaper in Southern Pines. I almost had a coronary when I saw it myself.

May all you readers enjoy this mishmash of my writings just as I enjoyed those old books from my mom and dad's library! Hot damn! Ain't life grand!

Bill Lindau
October 2013

voices

OF a

SanDHiLLS
BaBY BOOMeR

POEMS
&
SONG LYRICS

Undying Heartfire

Stooped over now with a head full of grey
a Hepburn-y quake as you talk
ever so slowly we move as we walk
and think of old times with each passing day

You play with your grandchildren
going to bed at eight
head full of family, friends here no more
memories of such a sweet weight

But with everything Father Time wrought upon you
He left you with such beauty and such charm
slender as ever and every time we meet
you pierce me through the heart

with your voice and your tender eyes so warm

Teen Athlete to a Scholar-Mother

A raven-haired beauty
with mind and heart of gold
sixteen and soft-spoken
though you played one no-nonsense tennis game

Now everyone calls you doctor
leading your corps of professors
and bringing up three sprightly ebony-haired children

Good-looking then, good-looking now
beautiful brain and a loving touch
gracefully mature no matter what age

Behind the Quiet

You're petite, shy,
with schoolteacher glasses
I don't mind
I like it

You say hello when you pass by
but that says so much about you
breakroom blather befits you not at all
I don't mind
I think it's cool

One day as I bought some kind of trinket from you
I found something about you to say
you talked and you talked
and you talked
before duty called again
I didn't mind
I loved it

Shoppers

Chance meeting at work
everything around us vanished
as we talked about flowers and the sun

Then someone marched up to me
asking about a petty issue
oh well, my job to put out such fires

I sorted them out
but you had already gone away—
that's the chilly unromantic world for you

But it warmed my day
you coming out from that impassive crowd

Enchanting Wild

Howling banshee
lioness on a hare
pouncing upon me
how long before she swallows me whole?

Wild one screams my name
spinning me round
angel or devil gripping my hands

Now I know you again
my sweet friend from bygone days
melting my heart with your ever-enchanting gaze

With You
(Song Lyrics)

You came to my life like a blooming May flower
into my world with such beautiful things
but the mean nasty world turned your garden so sour
now all that you hear are the bells of doom ringing

Quiet your tongue now with little to feed it
dim your eyes now with no beauty to see
gone are the people when you really need them
nothing to lean on—nobody but me

I'll stay by your side when all others take cover
stand by your children, your animals so dear
I'll stand by you as you mourn your sweet mother
Whatever you do, just remember, I'm here!

 (Repeat last line, lento)

All I Have Left of You

Remembering a kiss unexpected
squeezing my hand
hugs of hello and goodbye
a high-school portrait thirty-five-years old

They ask what you meant to me
show us they say: they look at you
smiling in your high-school yearbook
all I have left of you

How you kissed me as you parked your yellow car
the walk we took downtown
gentle talking as we enjoyed the colors of the fall

How bad I felt when I knew I'd angered you
how my heart soared when you said hello to me
welcome home longtime friend
farewell my lovely one

How I love you now and how I miss you badly
what I have left of you
memories of you squeezing my hands
the walk in the autumn rain

How you kissed me as you parked your yellow car
how you smile at me eternally from your yearbook
all I have left of you
but giving me much, much more!

To a Deceased Friend

Lovely you looked the day you said goodbye
before grey hair and sallow skin set in
No matter how often the sun rides across the sky
I always remember your loveliness, my dear

Autumn Rain
In Memoriam:
A Lovely Woman Gone Too Young
(Song Lyrics)

You were just sixteen when you graced my life
you smiled a dimply smile
Your gentle voice
floating on the August breeze

Your tender kisses tamed my heart
and with your winning guile
You took me in your loving arms
and set my soul at ease

Refrain:

We walked in the autumn rain
our love blooming like the flowers
As I walk through the autumn rain
my love for you blooms still

Second verse

You lost your heart to another man
he took you far from me
But I blessed you
as he took your loving hand

You went your ways and I went mine
I faded from your shade
My beard grew white from Father Time
Before I learned your fate

Refrain:

We walked in the autumn rain
our love blooming like the flowers
As I walk through autumn rain
my love for you blooms still

Third verse

One day you ceased to walk the earth
but many years went by
Before I learned of that awful day
and I hung my head and cried

I walk through autumn leaves alone
I wonder why you left
Too few years you were here and gone
so few years I have left me

Then I look into the greying clouds
I see your dimply smile
Rememb'ring when you were just sixteen
with all your winning guile

Refrain:

We walked in the autumn rain
our love blooming like the flowers
As I walk through autumn rain
my love for you blooms still

Love Through Fire and Ice
(Song Lyrics)

Oh, how good it feels to have you hold me
after all these years!
How long we've known each other
both in laughter and in tears.
I've known you at your ugliest
and at your very best
but soon I learned to bury the bad
and embrace the lovely rest

At first I didn't like you
when you blew into my town
my best friend fell for you
and I felt sure you'd cut him down.
But I saw what you did for him
that no one else could do
You gave his life such meaning
when he fell in love with you

Together you felt the fires of hell
You fought back to the fold
but something died along the way
and soon your love turned cold.
It grieved me when you left him
You were both my loving friends
But from the ruins came two new lives
for you that can never end

Such time has passed
Now I've returned
to the place where first we met
as beautiful as ever now
with a heart I'll not forget.
Time has set the silver on our heads
but forged us hearts anew
new life is running through my veins
now that I know I love you

a fiery blood flows from my heart
as I tell you I love you

Do You Love Me, Old Friend?

We met as wild and reckless youths
Now backaches and grandkids have entered our lives
yet still you remain one of my best friends

You've wanted to stay friends
And I respect your wish
yet my heart ran away from me

I never told you I love you
Never dreamed of it
but now I want to so badly

Do you love me, too?
I yearn to know
yet I fear to know

Will you let me make you happy?
Can you not return my feelings
as much as we have seen?

I hope you feel the same way
If not I'll face the world as best I can
and I will still love you

OK to Keep Mum

She no longer writes him
as much as she used to

He thinks he knows the reason
they had a good rapport
him and his longtime friend
they could talk all day about anything

She loves him
he knows she's not telling him something
she thinks it will destroy him
but he knows what it is

As he tries to pack up his disappointment
and leave it on the curb—he loves her, too
but knowing what she's not telling him
he knows when he has to move on

To save his heart
to save his love for her

Princess Home

Carolina Princess
with long flaxen tresses
I saw you sail by
in such days I thought you more worthy
of one much more noble than I

Years stream by like the ever-rolling river
and with them the long-lost past
but out of the mist you come
now from the west you fly so fast
the Carolina Princess returns now to her throne

She Returns

You don't know me
pardon me for ogling you
you're so nice looking
I try to be discreet
stealing glances as I chat on my cell phone
as you sit with your granny and all her friends

The more I try to stop glancing
the more I can't help noticing
so much about you
the long black hair
clear skin so fair

How much you make me think of her
old enough to be your mother
if she walked the earth today

a
SHORT
STORY

The Girl with the Dirty Face

*First published in Colonnades magazine
Elon College, North Carolina
Spring 1982*

PART I

"Hey, Shirley!" Mary Lou called from the meat section.

"Oh, no," I thought. "She's up to her old tricks." I went over there anyway, to see what she wanted.

Mary Lou Walsh was my best and only friend at the time, since I was new in town. She lived on a tobacco farm five miles from town and never went home until late in the evening. A fat, acne-faced girl, she was not much of a talker until she met me. And the day we met we were on an instant rapport. I loved her except for one thing: She was a compulsive shoplifter. Not a kleptomaniac, but close to it, she couldn't go into a store without taking something. She got her kicks that way and she tried many times to talk me into it too. When she called me over to the meat section just then, I saw that familiar gleam in her eyes.

Grinning, she pointed to a package of two-pound steaks. "Mary Lou," I said, "You're going to get locked up one of these days."

"Hey, don't you be getting off on no sermon again," she said. "You don't want your mama and daddy to have a nice big steak supper before they see that F it's up to you. Less you got money for it."

21

I'd just flunked algebra for the semester. A's and B's in everything except that. Dad knew it was my worst subject, but that F was something he wouldn't stand for. I wanted to take General Math, but he said no. That's for dummies, he said, and it wouldn't get me into the state university, where he'd taught English before he took a much higher position at the community college in Pine Hill. His dream, from the day I was born, was to send me to the state university. The first-born. A girl, but still the first born. So what Mary Lou said just now hit me right between the eyes.

Mary Lou was supposed to eat with us that evening. Mom, I knew, was racking her brains figuring out what to have. The sight of those steaks in the package, deep red with blood at the bottom, gave me an idea. I knew how Dad would react to my F, and I learned from Mom that a good way to soften him up for such news was to feed him a steak such as I saw. Get the steaks and cook them yourself; so something for Mom too.

I fished through my purse, my coat, wherever I carried money. Unfortunately I hadn't planned on any shopping; we were in the store mainly to pass the time and I didn't want to face Dad so soon. All I found was fifty-three cents. In the early 1960s that bought two Cokes and a pack of gum. Give Dad a Coke. No way. That wouldn't stave off what I saw coming. Three hours of screaming and yelling, then the silent treatment for two days. The silent treatment was much, much worse. I loved Dad and whenever I made him mad I felt like jumping off a bridge.

"What about it, Shirl?" asked Mary Lou. "I know you're a good girl and you don't go in for stealing, but don't you think it'd be a good thing?"

"You go ahead," I said. "I'll wait outside."

I glanced back at the package. There were twenty others like it. That was a lot of meat and the Quickie Mart wasn't hurting. A new section, a delicatessen, was being added.

Mary Lou had described the thrill she got from stealing food. Go ahead just this once, Shirley. Pay them the next time you go to the store.

Mary Lou caught me by the shoulder as I started out. "Hey, I ain't got anything big enough," she said, opening her denim jacket. "They know me too good besides. You're new here and you got that purse and that coat. The most I could get's a few candy bars."

She shrugged. "Course, I ain't makin' you do it, it's up to you. You wanna take it or not?"

A shiver of excitement, of fear, shot up my spine. I nodded to Mary Lou and she whispered her plan in my ear.

She took my money and I walked up and down the rear of the store until there was nobody in sight. Then, my heart beating so loud I thought somebody would hear, I strode hurriedly over to the package. A trickle of sweat was making its way down my forehead. I whisked up the package and crammed it into my inside coat pocket. All this was done in two seconds. Mary Lou was on her way to the counter and I unbuttoned my coat to hide the bulge.

I walked briskly, just fast enough to get out without looking suspicious. Mary Lou was at the counter with two Cokes by the time I was at the door. I was going to make it.

I was opening the door when I heard, "Hey you!" My heart was pierced by a knife. I threw open the door and ran. Let Mary Lou meet me at the house. I zipped around the corner of the building and looked for the nearest place to hide. Oh, why did I let her talk me into this? I saw some trees, and was halfway to them when I felt the manager's hand on my shoulder. He spun me around to an about-face.

"Give it here, kid," he said thickly. He was a skinny, baby-faced man of about thirty.

My eyes to the ground, I sighed and gave him the meat, my hand quivering like a leaf in a hundred-mile wind. I was going to die at fourteen. "I'm sorry," I whispered.

"Don't deny it, I saw you in there." He shook his head and clucked. "A pretty young thing like you, getting into this sort of thing. Why?"

"I don't know," I choked. I was afraid I was going to burst into tears, out there in the parking lot. "Look," I said in a shaking voice, "Just let me go, I'll pay for it later and I won't come back again. Please."

He looked at me stonily. "Did you read that sign?"

"What sign?" I'd read it, but I didn't want him to know. Mary Lou was nowhere in sight. Traitor!

"About shoplifters being prosecuted." He shoved the package under his arm as if it were an umbrella. "I mean it," he said in a heavy Southern accent. "I've had trouble with young thieves since I opened this store and I ain't sparing you 'cause you're so young and pretty. You come with me." He jerked me by the arm.

"I'm not the . . ."

"Hey Leroy!" he yelled. "Gotta go, I got another one!"

"Sir, I'm not the type that steals all the time!" I whined as he pulled me to a blue Impala. Southern accents and blue Impalas.

"Shut up, kid!" he yanked open the door and shoved me inside. I landed on my hip, on the point of the bone. "You're hurting me!" I cried.

He threw himself into the driver's seat and took off screeching tires as if he were Lee Marvin on "M Squad."

"What's your name?"

"Susan Davis," I stammered.

"Yeah, and I'm President Kennedy's grandfather.

"Come on, what's your name?"

"Susan Davis."

He sighed and gave me the most murderous look I'd ever seen. "Okay, Susan Davis," he said after a minute. "Your father will tell me your real name soon enough."

Oh why did I get into this? I saw myself in an endless chain of prisons, Shirley Patricia Donahue, larceny. Started her life of crime at fourteen. Daughter of an English professor at Pine Hill Community College. Disgrace to the Donahue family. Dirty thieving mick bitch. I tried to choke back the tears, shook my head to get them out of my eyes.

The man kept his eye on me. I had a faint hope that he'd take pity on me. Stony as ever, still. Sometimes I could soften Dad's heart with my tears, but never this man's.

"I don't have any sympathy for you," he said. "You're getting what you deserve." He must have felt like a real he-man whenever he turned in a shoplifter.

I looked out the window. There were some woods on my side. Pine trees under a graying sky.

"You married?" I asked the man.

"No," he said, puzzled. "Why'd you ask me that?"

I shrugged. "Just making conversation."

"Oh," he said. "I thought about it a bunch of times, but I never found the right one. Had a nice time looking, though."

As he was talking, I reached over and pulled the

key out of the ignition and held it up. The car began to slow down. "Why, you little bitch!" he yelled. "Gimme that key!"

My heart beating much louder and faster now, I threw the key at the back seat, rammed open the door and tumbled out. I must have somersaulted three times on the hard gravel before I sprang up on my feet and cut out for the woods like the proverbial bat out of hell. I heard him yelling as the car stopped and I made my dash for the woods. I was crashing into trees, my back and hips burning where I'd landed, limbs and bushes tearing at me, my lungs about to explode, wanting to stop but knowing I couldn't, running and running and running and everything else be damned.

The light was still on in my father's study. It was the middle of the night and it was starting to rain. All over I was sore and numb from the cold and the pain. I'd torn my hose to shreds and had to keep kicking my legs to put life back into them, keep them from falling off. On top of that I was catching cold. I sneezed, pinching my nose to muffle it. My hand was sticky and slimy from snot.

I didn't give a damn now; all I wanted was a place to stay, at least until morning. Try running away from home when you're a fourteen-year-old girl and it's the goddamn middle of January. You hide out all night and you don't have any food or any money (was I going to pop that Mary Lou Walsh!) and you'd bet your right arm everybody was out looking for you. Your family, the police, the FBI and the Marines. I imagined how Bonnie and Clyde must have felt. I was Bonnie without a Clyde.

I'd made my way home, crawling through back

yards and clumps of bushes and trees. If you had seen me when I got to the house, you might have mistaken me for Tarzan's Jane. Jane with a ragged coat, ribboned stockings on my legs. Long, brown hair stringing with mud, sand, pine needles, body odor that could have killed a moose.

I was going to split into that basement. Go to my room in the morning, when Dad was at the college and Mom was taking my little brothers to school. Bathe and change, pack a bag and get as far away as I could. Christ, I wished I could cry some more.

I took off my shoes and the remains of my stockings, and edged inside the basement door. Not a sound in the house, but I knew Dad was up; he and Mom were most likely pacing the floor and waiting to hear from the police. More jittery than a cat in front of a German Shepherd. Who was the cat and who was the German Shepherd?

In the basement I unrolled a mattress Dad kept there, and lowered myself down onto it. What had Mary Lou done? Did she come over and confess everything? Why did I let her talk me into something so stupid? Maybe, I thought wryly, when her crimes caught up with her we'd see each other in the same home for wayward girls.

I wanted to purge myself, to cry or to puke. But I couldn't cry anymore. I tried sticking my fingers down my throat, but I couldn't even do that; I hadn't eaten since lunchtime, I remembered.

Instead I turned over and stared at the pilot light over my head. Think of nothing but the pilot light flickering, as you might sit at a campfire and stare at the flames.

I was half-asleep when the basement door opened and the light came on.

PART II

Patrick Donahue was a lion in a cage as he paced the floor of his study and shakily massaged his hands. A folder of papers, half of them ungraded, lay open on his desk. This was no time to grade any papers, he thought, not after this night. He would remember this night as long as he lived. After the hassle with the Quickie Mart and the police, it was a strain to try to appear as though nothing was wrong in front of Errin and Patrick Jr. His two little sons had been asking all evening where Shirley was before his wife finally put them to bed. Donahue always had the same answer, "She's spending the night with a friend," although he could barely contain his anxiety or his anger from his sons.

His hair and goatee were flecking with grey as he got closer to fifty. He was getting a paunch, too, even though he kept himself fit by jogging two miles a day and lifting weights in the basement. Still, in his state he wouldn't be surprised if he dropped dead tonight of a heart attack.

Donahue and his wife Teresa knew the whole story. Teresa had called Mary Lou Walsh at her house and the girl broke down in tears telling everything: Shirley's F in algebra, Mary Lou talking her into stealing the steaks, the manager taking Shirley away. When he heard this, Donahue seized the phone and threatened to call the police if he every saw Mary Lou around his daughter again.

He then called the Quickie Mart and got the rest of the story from Tommy Fields, the manager. After Shirley had run, Fields had gone to the police and taken out a warrant, but the police had not found her yet. When

Donahue told Fields to drop the charges, Fields refused. "I gotta get tough around my place, Jack," he said. "I don't care whose kid she is. Young kids clean me out right and left and anybody I catch, they're gonna pay but good."

"You don't call off that warrant," Donahue yelled over the phone, "I'm coming down there right now."

"You go right ahead," the man retorted.

Over Teresa's protests, Donahue took off in the car. He spent at least thirty minutes talking to Fields, who would settle for nothing less than Shirley's arrest. Donahue felt as if he were a defense attorney arguing before a vindictive judge. Finally he picked up the phone, called the police station and shoved the phone at Fields. "Tell them you're calling it off," said Donahue.

"No, buddy—now, I gotta take a stand."

"Call it off," Donahue growled, "Or I'll get her a lawyer and fight this thing to the end! I mean it!"

Fields hemmed and hawed a few minutes. Apparently the English professor wasn't bluffing. He took he phone gingerly from Donahue's hand and stammered into the phone to drop the charges. "I've been talking to the girl's father," he added. Then he handed back the phone.

Donahue gave the police some vital information on his daughter, for the desk sergeant to put on Missing Persons. Then he left the store. "Don't ever let your brat in here again!" Fields yelled after him.

At the station Donahue had spent another thirty minutes giving out information on Shirley and signing the necessary papers. He also gave the police a few tips on dealing with the girl. He would take care of her himself.

Boy, would he take care of her! A beautiful girl with her brains! Ivy League material! Now, as if that F wasn't enough, she just had to go and do one more stupid thing that could blow her whole thing beyond redemption. And it would really make him look good, the people at the college knowing he had a child in trouble for stealing. He'd back her up, but she would surely pay for it.

Teresa came in as he was pacing the floor. She was in nightgown and curlers and had gone to bed two hours ago. "Are you still up?" she said. "You'll wake the boys pacing the floor like that."

"No word yet," he said. "The police haven't called."

"Would you give them time?" she whined. "If they don't call, she'll come home herself. Anyway, Pat," she added, "sitting up fretting like this is not going to bring her back. Maybe she's just staying with one of her friends, as you told Errin and Pat, and she's waiting for you to cool off. I know how she is."

"If she's staying with that Mary Lou Walsh I'll …"

"Calm down! It's talk like that that keeps her away. I certainly don't blame her for being so frightened, hearing you."

She had talked him out of calling the police every thirty minutes. Quit hassling them, give them time. Give her time. If they didn't hear from the police or Shirley the next day, call them then. But not before.

Twelve noon was a long time from now, Donahue thought. In the morning he would call a substitute and go look for Shirley himself. Oh that child! She would really catch it when he found her.

Teresa grabbed him as he started pacing the floor again. "I am not going to stay up," she said, "and have you do that all night. Go to the basement, lift your weights. That should make you feel better."

Donahue went downstairs. He made himself a cup of tea in the kitchen, pouring in a healthy shot of Irish whiskey for good measure. What he really wanted was to get drunk.

While he waited for the tea to cool, he went back upstairs and offered Teresa some. "No," she said, and he came back down.

He drank the tea. The creamy, burning drink took some of the heat off him. Not all, though. When that girl comes back she's really going to get it …

He remembered his younger sister Eunice, who left home when she was fifteen. Neither he nor his elder sister nor their parents ever heard from her again. One day Eunice cut school with her boyfriend, and was driving to the beach, but a truant officer caught her in a store. The officer took her home and Donahue's father, a quick-tempered, beefy construction foreman, was in a drunken rage and took after her with his belt. When he got through, Eunice's arms and legs were spotted black and blue and green. The girl cried for three hours in young Donahue's arms, until she fell asleep.

Eunice was gone the next morning. She'd slipped out, in the middle of the night, with a valise and three dresses. Patrick was the last one in the family to see her, asleep, her face red and swollen, her arms and legs spotted with bruises. Then she was gone.

Graveyard thoughts, Donahue thought. Shirley is certainly going to learn a lesson.

He drained his cup, and made himself another one.

After a third cup, Donahue decided to take Teresa's advice. He was feeling the whiskey, but that didn't make him feel any better. Forty times with the barbell, as drunk as he was, and he should feel good and tired. In the morning he'd go about as he had planned. Four in the morning and still no trace of his daughter. The silence in the house, the phone that sat there not ringing was unnerving. *Shirley get home, goddamn you.*

He opened the basement door and turned on the light. Something down there started rustling. "Don't move, whoever you are!" he called.

The rustling stopped. Donahue picked up a hammer that was hanging on the wall and inched down the steps. "Don't try anything," he called, his voice thick with the whiskey. "I've a hammer here and I don't want any trouble. Now you come to the steps where I can see you."

Her bare feet dirty, her dark red coat wrinkled, torn and equally filthy, her face sullen and sheepish and hair matted and tangled, she slinked to the foot of the steps. "It's me, Father," she whispered.

The girl was looking at the ground, her neck exposed as if she were expecting a headsman's axe.

An image flashed through Donahue's mind: His father going after his sister Eunice with his belt, hacking at her with swift, brutal strokes. The scream of the agonized girl as a blow caught her on the hip and catapulted her over a chair …

Donahue slumped against the wall and shook his head.

After a minute he straightened up and started down the stairs, the hammer still in his hand. Shirley looked up at him, her blue eyes like those of a doe at bay, resigned to the fate she saw coming.

Her father stopped. He dropped the hammer and it fell clunking down the steps. Shirley watched it fall, a look of bewilderment in her eyes.

Patrick Donahue's mouth, lined by the goatee that Shirley had often called a devil's beard, broke into a grin.

Slowly, painfully, Shirley took two steps up. Her father lifted his right hand up to her face. It was smeared, streaked with tears and dirt and snot, but it was still beautiful.

memoirs
&
eulogies

Dog About Town

It was love at first sight between Pug and me, in the summer of 1968.

Pug was a golden retriever. He lived in Southern Pines, North Carolina when I was in high school. His owner, or rather, the person he was registered under, lived a few blocks from me. The dog never really belonged to any one person, however. Pug belonged to the person he took a fancy to at the time.

At fifteen, I was one of those people.

When I met Pug, I already had a dog, a Chihuahua named Pancho. He and Pug became friends. When Pancho got hit by a car and killed, Pug continued to visit us.

Pug did not have a bashful bone in his body. He made friends quickly with both the two-legged and four-legged. He made himself at home wherever he went.

The first time I let him into my house, he bounded straight up the stairs and into my mother's bed—with my mother in it.

"I was sound asleep until he came in," my mother said later. "But I almost had a coronary when this enormous thing jumped into bed with me."

My father nicknamed him "The Yellow Peril," a misnomer if there ever was one. Pug never bit anyone.

Pug loved children, too. Many of the neighborhood kids came to play with him and swing on the Tarzan rope I had in a tree in my yard. Pug even let the smaller children ride him.

Once a ten-year-old girl named Peggy was climbing the rope, not high enough to get hurt if she fell. Peggy had almost reached the branch when Pug took the loose end of the rope in his mouth and engaged the tree in a tug-of-war.

Our damsel in distress held on as tight as she could, wide-eyed with fright as the rope bucked and jumped in the dog's mouth. Her friend Jodi writhed on the ground with helpless laughter, before I finally pried the rope from Pug's mouth.

Although his real owner was not especially strait-laced, Pug hated alcohol and cigarette smoke. He always left the room when someone lighted a cigarette. Not only did he shy away from the smell of alcohol, but he'd even back away from an unopened bottle.

Pug was strictly a landlubber. I found this out the hard way, when three of us tried to teach him how to swim one Sunday at Highland Trails Lake. Steve and Bobby threw Pug into the water, where I was swimming. The first thing our terrified pupil did was thrash and paddle for the nearest floating object—me.

Pug clawed and flailed at my back, forcing me under to get free of his flying nails, until Steve dove in and pulled the struggling bundle of legs back to shore. That was Pug's first swimming lesson. His last, too.

My father inadvertently discovered the power of Pug's biological compass, when he took the dog to Fayetteville one afternoon. My father got into a fender-bender at a downtown traffic light. The accident spooked Pug. He jumped out of the car and ran away. My father could not get him to come back. The dog had run out of sight. After an hour's search, Dad gave up and went home.

Fearing the worst, we took out a lost-and-found ad in three newspapers. Two afternoons later, Pug was waiting for me when I came home from school. I still cannot figure out how he made it back, whether a motorist picked him up or he walked the rest of the way back.

Pug had an unswerving loyalty to those with whom he took up. If we were not careful about leaving the house for school and work, my father, my mother or I would find thirty pounds of dog on our heels. If we kept him in the house while we all made our getaway, Pug would claw and scamper around until he found a way out.

He knew the sounds of both my parents' cars: The roar of my mother's 1964 Ford Falcon and the putter of my father's Toyota. Both sounds meant it was close to dinnertime. In the morning, the sound of the cars fading away in the distance only made Pug that much more frantic to catch up with his owners.

It did not take Pug too long to learn where I went to school or where my parents worked. Three times I gazed outside the classroom window, only to find "The Yellow Peril" whining and pawing at the entrance. Once, when he decided to hang out with Dad, Pug waited for him at the door to his office. He drew a complaint from the boss for drooling on the doorknob.

One of Pug's favorite playgrounds was the lawn outside my mother's office, where he ran around and chased squirrels, or sat on the front steps greeting customers like a living marble lion—a bounding, drooling mountain lion.

Except for my father's boss, Pug made friends quickly with the others at work, the ones Dad made contact with. Once the members of the town council let the dog set in on one of their meetings that Dad covered. When the council took a vote on an issue, Pug gave out his assent with a splendid bark.

Pug disappeared four months after I started college. Nobody knows what happened to him. It was a long time, however, before anybody believed Pug had gone to his eternal reward. For all we knew, he simply chose a new master. That's what we kept telling ourselves.

"The Yellow Peril" may be gone, but nobody has forgotten him. After all these years, my friends and I—the ones who are still around, that is—laugh about the time we taught that poor canine to swim, and terrorizing the school and the local newspaper to be with his new buddies.

Farewell to My Crazy Old Friend

Eulogy for Gary Farrell Sessoms
(1953-2009)
One of the first friends I made when we moved
to Southern Pines, North Carolina.

Delivered at his funeral service.

Gary, I didn't know you as long as some of the people here today, but you were one of my best and oldest friends in the world. I came to The Pines more than 40 years ago, and you made me feel right at home.

We cut up in class together, drove teachers and parents nuts, but it was the harmless kind of wild, the kind that hurts nobody in the long run. You were a holy terror on the football field and we watched a lot of your games.

You never let your achievements go to your head. You respected friends and strangers alike, and you never thought you were better than anybody else. Except for a few months running track in ninth grade, I didn't have much of an athletic career, but that didn't matter to you, you always remained my friend no matter what I did.

Younger people say, "I have your back." Nobody put it that way when you and I were that age, but I can honestly say you certainly had mine.

After high school, we went our different ways and we didn't see each other that much. We both came and went in The Pines, going to all sorts of different places and getting into all sorts of different things. But whether we got together or not, I was always sure of one thing; you were still my friend.

I mourned for your beloved brother Gene, because I liked him, too, and I knew you loved him, and I was glad to be there for you, just as you have always been there for me.

You went away thirteen years ago and I never saw you again. But I knew you'd come back sometime. As far as I was concerned, you never left.

Your family today is mourning the loss of a fabulous son, stepson, brother and father. And so many of us in this room are mourning the loss of one of the best friends we ever had.

Sooner or later, the Lord will call the rest of us back to Him. We know when that time comes, you and Gene will be at the gates to greet each and every one of us. Until that time, Gary, we will all miss you so very much. Our friend, our brother.

A Blue Knight in Red Devil Country:
An Old Rival's Affection for Aberdeen

In 1969, I would never have believed I would be writing for a magazine devoted to Aberdeen as well as Southern Pines. I lived in Southern Pines during my teens, and off and on after that, and to this day I remain fiercely patriotic about Southern Pines.

But that doesn't mean we didn't find anything about our Aberdeen neighbors to love—such as several clothing stores, a nice movie house that showed the current popular films, a Dairy Queen, and a popular lake to cool off in during the summer.

Aberdeen Lake, in fact, makes up a large part of my memories of the first summer I spent in Moore County. I moved to the Sandhills from Winston-Salem in the fall of 1966, just as I was starting eighth grade. In those days, when the towns had their own school systems, I only knew one youth from Aberdeen, a classmate who transferred to East Southern Pines High School after he had gotten into a bit of trouble at Aberdeen.

Aberdeen and Southern Pines also had their own newspapers: *The Pilot* and the *Sandhill Citizen*, two weeklies. *The Pilot* is still in existence, printing twice a week. The *Sandhill Citizen* evolved into a daily publication called the *Citizen News-Record*, before it folded early in 1996.

Those who have moved to the Sandhills since 1980 may have hardly any idea of what relations were like between the two towns. With a smaller population, fewer businesses and, as I noted before, two separate school systems and two different newspapers, the citizens of Southern Pines and Aberdeen stuck to themselves more, unless they had jobs in other towns.

Another huge difference: Southern Pines had more golf courses than Aberdeen did, while Aberdeen had a larger industrial area—chiefly manufacturing.

I also came of age in the days when most of the time you could walk to everything. All the major businesses and food and clothing stores, the pharmacies, doctors and dentists, police, fire departments, town hall, post offices and the schools, were mostly within walking distance in both Southern Pines and Aberdeen.

I remember this part of local history from an adolescent's-eye view, especially the athletic rivalries between Aberdeen and East Southern Pines high schools.

It was like that between U.N.C. and N.C. State. The Blue Knights (East Southern Pines) and Red Devils (Aberdeen) scheduled their games at the end of the regular season—the top rivalry in the conference. Southern Pines won the last two football games between the two schools in the fall of 1967 and 1968.

The fights after the games between Aberdeen and Southern Pines were part of local lore. They usually took place whenever the two groups of kids encountered each other at one of the popular eateries along U.S. 1. I was more of a peace-loving kid than most of my friends, so I never got into any of the fights myself.

At East Southern Pines, we had our own images of the Aberdeen residents, and it was not too flattering, so I won't go into it. I have no doubt the Aberdeen High students had the same stereotypes of Southern Pines kids.

In the summer of 1969 some kids in Southern Pines would hang around the town park, predicting what would happen when Pinecrest opened and the kids from the different schools in Pinehurst, Southern Pines, Aberdeen and West End got together. There would be fights all over the place.

They were wrong.

As a matter of fact, many of the kids from different schools became close friends. Once they played football and basketball together and joined the same clubs, we all put aside our differences and decided those other folks weren't so bad after all. We all went to parties together, and I still count a lot of past and present Aberdeen residents among my closest friends.

Even before the schools opened, I went to Aberdeen a lot. I got my first job in the Aberdeen town limits, at Hardee's. I bought a lot of clothes from the merchants downtown and saw many a movie at the Town and Country Cinema (which, sad to say, has just closed). Among these movies were "The Dirty Dozen," "Bonnie and Clyde," "You Only Live Twice," and "Romeo and Juliet."

Some of us Southern Pines kids even rode our bicycles to Aberdeen Lake. I remember riding along with one of my more athletic friends, in the middle of July. It wore me out trying to keep up with him. We rode them on the main drag, too; I wouldn't dare attempt that now. Aberdeen, we see, has changed a lot since then. The Dairy Queen folded about 30 years ago; the Aberdeen Law Enforcement Center is now on that site. At least two of the clothing and shoe stores I often patronized have closed, and these kinds of businesses are now out in various malls—far beyond walking distance. Since 2012, Aberdeen has had an online newspaper, *The Aberdeen Times*, for its local media outlet.

The change is not all bad. The town has its own recreation department, and at least one art gallery and one music store. There are some good places to eat and shop along the main drag.

Some things have remained, however. The lake is still a popular recreation area, with a fabulous evening celebration and fireworks show on the Fourth of July. Then there is the annual Malcolm Blue Festival in the fall.

If you ever think your hometown is as dull as proverbial ditchwater, take a closer look. Every place, big or small, harbors plenty of good tales. Check it all out!

Luv-a-Horse!

A childhood allergy kept me away from riding horses as much as I wanted to, but I still love those magnificent beasts and I have had my adventures and misadventures on them. While I love Westerns and historical war movies (and especially Alfred, Lord Tennyson's classic poem "Charge of the Light Brigade"), I am glad most armies no longer use them because they've died in battle along with the people they serve.

Whenever I'm driving through the country, on a back road, I love to stop and talk to any horses I see by the side of the road. They rival the dog as man's best friend, and they even have therapeutic value.

I didn't ride any for years, between my early teens and the past few years. My most recent experiences on horseback occurred at a street festival in St. Pauls, North Carolina. A horse owner offered three-minute pony rides, on a turnstile. Although I was two or three times the size of most of his young customers, he let me ride Nugget, his pony.

The first time I tried to mount was a bust. I couldn't quite make it on the cute little horse's back. So I gave up, before I broke one or both our necks.

I came back a year later, in 2010. This time was a success, as I paid much more attention to the owner's instructions.

I can't recall ever getting so much as a little three-minute pony ride until a few years ago. It reminded me of the first time I ever rode a horse—on a trail, that is.

At age fourteen I went to a stable in Southern Pines. They were conducting trail rides. My mount was a gelding named Helpmate.

Halfway down the trail he bolted. I guess he'd had his fill of inept city slickers climbing on his back all day. He hauled ass back to the stable and there was no way I could make him stop. At least twice he rode me smack-dab into some overhanging branches, but that was nothing compared to when he crossed the road, and I was sure we were going to get hit by a car.

Anybody ever see a 1962 Kirk Douglas film called "Lonely are the Brave"? He plays a cowboy who just got out of prison and decides to run from the law again. I won't go into the ending, but that's what I thought of atop this living, whinnying juggernaut, dodging cars on May Street.

Helpmate didn't stop until he went back to his stall. He kept on running, and I think this was the first time I recall making a snap judgment that was right. At first I held my arms out to stop him at the stable gate. He kept on going.

Right before I would've collided with the top of the gate, I ducked down. People who saw that just about freaked. They were sure that in three seconds I'd be splattered all over that gate like proverbial strawberry jam (Christopher Plummer in "Battle of Britain"). Funny thing. It wasn't enough to make me swear off riding. I rode a few more times that year. I still get into it occasionally.

You hear of equine therapy programs for troubled kids. There's one in Lumber Bridge. I can imagine how much somebody would love riding one of those beautiful animals.

Lately I watched a beautiful, heart-warming horse movie, a 2005 indie film called "The Colt." It stars Ryan Merriman as a Union cavalryman whose mare gives birth in the middle of a Civil War skirmish. His superior officers order him to get rid of the colt, but he cannot bring himself to kill the animal, and both his sergeant and the captain have a change of heart about it, too. The baby horse becomes the company mascot, captivating everyone who sees it, including the enemy. Several people whom I have talked into seeing this movie have fallen in love with it, too, just as the Civil War soldiers with the title character.

Now motorized vehicles have literally put horses out to pasture. But people still love to ride them, bet on their races and other things. I always enjoy their company in the middle of a long country drive. Such gentle giants. What would we do without them?

Dad's War Stories

*(To the gentleman who taught me
a guy doesn't have to throw punches
to be a man.)*

As a veteran of World War II, my father had a lot
to say about the years 1942 to 1945. He served as a para-
trooper, and took part in the liberation of the Philippines.
He also served as a war correspondent.

William Edwin Lindau was a member of the 511th
Airborne, later a part of the 82nd Airborne Division. He
was awarded a Bronze Star and honorably discharged with
the rank of Staff Sergeant.

After the war, he became an editor for several
newspapers in North Carolina, including *The Asheville
Citizen* and *The Winston-Salem Journal*, but he never forgot
his wartime experience.

As a boy I had a romantic fascination with the mili-
tary and with World War II (I believe to this day it was
one of the few justified wars in our history, besides the
American Revolution). I watched Walter Cronkite's
"Twentieth Century" TV documentary, and read every
history book I could that dealt with the war. When I was
in fifth grade there was hardly a tank, warplane or period
of Hitler's life that I did not know about.

Our house was filled with mementos of Dad's tour
of duty in the Pacific. We had old copies of *Yank* maga-
zine and *Stars and Stripes*, jackets, boots, badges, a boxing
medal and his Bronze Star.

The item my father treasured the most was a cap-
tured Japanese flag. A Filipino boy had given it to him for
two candy bars. The flag belonged to a Japanese soldier

who had been killed at Manila.

Dad loved to tell me of his wartime adventures, though in later years I figured out it was more for his little boy's entertainment than of any pleasure he took in remembering what he experienced in combat.

One of his stories was about his drill sergeant in basic training. The drillmaster was a third-grade dropout who bawled out, after each roll call, "Goddamn all you men that ain't here! All you men that ain't here will report to me at 1700 hours."

Dad received that Bronze Star for saving a major's life in the Philippines. He said the major was paying a visit to the latrine. An enemy sniper almost caught the major with his pants down—literally—when Dad shot the sniper just as the sniper was drawing a bead on the Yank officer from a tree.

My father taught me the proper techniques of shooting, parachuting and throwing hand grenades (pull the pin, count to three, lob at the foe). I learned about keeping my backside down when advancing on a ma-chine-gun nest, and slam-dunking a pineapple grenade down the open hatch of a tank.

When we moved to Southern Pines from Winston-Salem, Dad took me to Fort Bragg all the time. This in-cluded visits to the Special Forces obstacle course and the John F. Kennedy Museum for Special Warfare, both in Fort Bragg.

When I was older, Dad told me two more war stories, in which he became convinced that Somebody Up There was in his corner.

"I was in a foxhole and two guys came in and forced me out of it," he said. "Soon the enemy started firing, and a mortar shell landed right in the foxhole. One of the guys was killed instantly, but it took the other one

52

ten minutes to die."

"Another time," he said, "A second lieutenant pulled rank on me to take my seat on a transport plane. I had to wait for the next one out. A few hours later that plane was reported missing over the North China Sea."

For all his war tales, Dad was the most peace-loving man I've ever known. He said sometimes you have to go to war to defend your way of life, but he never wanted his children to come any closer to war than a John Wayne movie.

"When you're in a foxhole and you've got bullets flying all around you, all that Ernest Hemingway stuff goes right out the window and all you want to do is stay alive."

In 1985, Dad commemorated the 40th anniversary of the war's end in his own special way. Knowing that his captured Japanese flag was one of the personal effects of a fallen soldier, Dad mailed the flag back to Japan. My father was not certain that the deceased soldier's relatives could be traced, or if any of them were still living, but he felt it was the best thing to do to celebrate the forty years of peace between the United States and Japan.

That December my father received a box from Japan. It contained a wooden geisha-girl doll. It was a gift from the deceased soldier's brother. The brother said in the accompanying letter that until he received the flag, the family had nothing in their loved one's memory. There was no mistaking the degree of gratitude in the letter; the surviving brother said that the flag was the best way the soldier could be honored.

The First Woman of My Life

She entered this world as Mary Elizabeth Sanders in 1919, the year Prohibition became the law of the land. God called her home ten days after the 9/11 attacks.

"Betsy" as her family called her, made a name for herself in the Sandhills of North Carolina, writing book reviews, serving in the local chamber of commerce and publishing two books celebrating her hometown of Southern Pines, where she and her husband spent the rest of their lives.

And for 49 years she was my best friend of all time.

She was born in Murfreesboro, Tennessee, to a pair of old-time Methodists. A year or two after she was born, they moved to Black Mountain, where her father took a job at the Blue Ridge Assembly, a religious retreat sanctioned by the YMCA. Her father, Herbert W. Sanders, served as executive director in the 1930s and 1940s, until he retired.

A baby sister, Sally, joined the family in 1926. At this writing, Mrs. Sally Blankenship resides in Asheville, in the same house in which she married railroad worker George Blankenship. They raised five children in their little home and I love her tremendously.

The oldest photo I remember of my mother showed a former baseball player and university professor named Paul Grist, holding the two-year-old toddler, standing upright in the palms of his outstretched hands at the Blue Ridge Assembly.

Herbert and Myra Bell Sanders lived in a cottage on the grounds with their two daughters. Betsy Sanders worked on the staff during high school and college, attending what is now the University of North Carolina in

Greensboro, graduating with a B.A. in art history in 1941.

I credit my mother with instilling a love of the arts in me. She kept many of her textbooks and continued to paint for many, many years, with oils, watercolors, polymers, pen and ink and others. My sister Sara still has most of our mother's paintings. Our mother didn't give a hoot about making a lot of money; she did it because she liked to do it.

She did sell her artwork at least once, when we lived in Winston-Salem. Her husband's friend Charlie Matthews gave me free lessons at his judo clinic for doing charcoal drawings of two of the sport's highest-ranking dignitaries (judo stars?). That was a good payment for me, and I had fun there.

Her art history textbooks were big, coffee-table beauties with color plates of the famous artworks from Greece, Rome, the Middle Ages, and the Renaissance to the present. I loved to look at those books when I was a child, though those Medieval and Renaissance paintings of Hell spooked me so much that I kept the lights on when I went to sleep. Luca Signorelli's "The Last Judgment," showing demons torturing naked sinners, was the worst.

But I loved those works all the same, and I took up painting myself.

There was no mistaking Betsy Sanders's politics; she was a New Deal Democrat to the hilt. She also told me later she believed in communism when she was in college. "Back then, the best people in the world were communists," she said.

She also told me about working with a German girl at the Blue Ridge Assembly. She said the girl was in the Hitler Youth, and believed Hitler would do good things at the time. This was long before most Americans thought Hitler was no worse than a harmless loudmouth. Betsy never heard from the girl again after she went back to Germany. In later years, Betsy wondered what became of her, how utterly disillusioned her sweet, pretty German friend must have felt when this odd man, so full of beautiful promises, brought the wrath of the world upon her people's heads.

My mother also talked a lot about the Great Depression, about the lean times everybody went through. She once said many of her male high-school classmates joined ROTC just to wear the uniforms, for an extra set of clothes and shoes.

At college, Betsy met a U.N.C-Chapel Hill student during a special performance. Wiliam Edwin Lindau played the clown in a show featuring his school's acrobatic team. They started dating, and in 1942, after he'd left school to work as a newspaper reporter, they got married.

Herb and Myra Bell Sanders were not terribly pleased over the rumors they heard about their daughter, such as her partying and her embrace of communism. "I should never have let you go away to college," her father once said to her.

It hardly thrilled them, too, when she brought her then-boyfriend (my father) home to meet her folks. Dating a Yankee (he was a native New Yorker who came down here to go to his father's old university) made for the ultimate scandal in the small Southern mountain town of Black Mountain.

With World War II raging, Betsy's young husband was drafted into the Army. He was sent to the Pacific, where he served until 1947. Late in 1944, my sister was born during his deployment.

After he came home from the war, the family moved around in the mountains, with dad writing for a paper in Waynesville, and then the *Asheville Citizen*. Late in

1952, a boy joined the family. Namely, yours truly.

We moved to Winston-Salem late in 1960, and late in 1966 we moved to Southern Pines, where my parents stayed to the end of their days; father in 1989, mom in 2001.

She went back to work shortly after we moved to what local folks call "The Pines." This is when she made a name for herself, and made a lot of friends. She wrote a weekly book column for *The Pilot*, and also worked at the Campbell House, on the Stoneybrook Steeplechase Committee, and at the Sandhills Area Chamber of Commerce.

In 1980, she edited a book titled "Young Southern Pines," a local history written by Helen Huttenhauer. Mom herself had a history of her own published seven years later, in a celebration of the Town of Southern Pines's centennial: "The First Hundred Years" in 1987.

You can't say enough about Betsy Sanders Lindau. She took her family obligations seriously from the day she and dad said their "I do's." She raised my older sister and me through thick and thin—even when we were being totally obnoxious and nobody else would have put up with either of us—through childhood, our rebellious teen years and up until we struck out on our own. And even beyond.

I'll never forget her sense of humor. For several years she and her parents made it a family thing to read the various books of Walt Kelly's famed "Pogo" comic strip aloud. When her parents went to their eternal reward (my grandmother passed in 1960, and grandpa Herb joined her in 1963), I joined in on the Pogo readings. If you read it aloud, taking the different parts as we did, it would really have you cracking up.

Mom and I continued to read the strip aloud by ourselves, dividing up the parts of the various denizens of the Okefenokee Swamp: Pogo, Albert the Alligator, Howland Owl, Churchy LaFemme, Ma'mzelle Hepzibah, Beauregard the Dog, a deacon badger, the three bats Bewitched, Bothered and Bemildred, and who knows who else. Many times we'd switch roles, but I always took Albert the Alligator's part, and also of his nephew Alabaster.

She and dad also loved Bill Cosby. They bought most if not all of his early record albums. Mom loved "Laugh-In" and "Saturday Night Live" and, later, "Monty Python."

Mom loved to tell funny stories about her children. Among the anecdotes I remember were my sister's expression when the baker's chocolate she started eating didn't match the taste she expected. After mom's repeated warnings, Sara (she was 15 at the time) defiantly put one of the bars in her mouth, and as she was chewing, said, "I likkke it." But the face sis made gave her away and she spat it out.

Mom never stopped talking about two of my misadventures. When I was five or six, we went to Mount Mitchell and I got stuck in one of those big wooden signs outside the lodge. I don't know what I was thinking, but I had climbed through the space between the slats. I was standing up and couldn't stoop down to slither back out. A ranger had to come and somehow pry me out of there.

When I was eleven we spent dad's vacation at Nag's Head. After I finished eating at one of the seafood restaurants, I went to the restroom. I couldn't turn the doorknob to get out of there, so I called for help. A big man walked by and opened the door, walking by without a word.

When I came back to the table, I asked my folks if they heard any muffled cries for help. A woman at the next table heard me and went into convulsions. We started cracking up, too, thankful for my silent, unknown savior.

We had our ups and downs during my younger years, but with time I learned to appreciate what a quality human being she was, going above and beyond the call of duty to help out my sister and me. I owe her a tremendous amount, which would take many lifetimes to pay back.

It is amazing how many people remember my dear departed momma after all this time. One of them, Sherri Brooks of Winston-Salem, was a little girl when we lived there. Her grandmother lived next door to us and she was one of mom's best friends. I friended Sherri on Facebook about two years ago. What a small, and often wonderful, world this is!

Even after so long in her grave, I still miss Betsy Sanders Lindau. You never "get over" the passing of your mother, or anybody else you love and cherish dearly. She and my father, and their parents and friends, are still around, looking after us from wherever they are and talking with their old friends about what a handful we all used to be.

R.I.P., Mother! I love you!

The Story of Little Chrissakes:
One Way to Make People Laugh—
Lose Your Temper

I wish I had five dollars for every time I cussed out somebody more than he/she deserved and felt silly for my outburst an hour or so later. You may feel good right after you do it, after such a buildup of frustrations, but when you cool off you start thinking you might have made a fool of yourself.

I think about all of us can use a little help keeping our cool at some time or another. I think the two best ways are to find a levelheaded, diplomatic way to tell the offending person what's made you so mad, and find a way to laugh at it sooner or later. Don't just stew about it too long or blow up at the slightest provocation.

I've learned the hard way what can happen when you let your temper get the better of you. You can get fired, drive your friends away, and the businesses and services you depend on will take their own sweet time getting around to you, because they'd rather not deal with you.

It can also take its toll on your health. Research reported in a Washington Post feature indicates the release of stress hormones from anger and other negative emotions can have such detrimental effects as suppressing the immune system and restricting blood vessels. This includes hormones such as adrenalin and cortisol, the ones that gear up the body in a "fight or flight" situation. In my own case, sometimes when I get upset over something, I'll start having an asthma attack. I've never had an asthma attack from a good mood.

And, as I said before, you can make a fool of yourself.

It's amazing how that kind of karma can work against you. Sometimes it can bite you in the tuchus at that very moment. Here are some instances I can think of, including one in which somebody put on the proverbial brakes in the nick of time.

Shortly after I finished high school, I had a little party on the basement of my parents' house. The gas heater hung from the ceiling, low enough to be at forehead level, with the grid in the living room where it generated heat. During this little get-together, "Linda" got mad at her boyfriend. The argument escalated to the point where Linda stood up and started walking out. As she was walking, she turned around to give "Alan" another salvo of abuse. Not looking where she was going, she hit her head on the metal corner of the heater.

Not that I took pleasure in anybody getting hurt on the family property, but I think it's the worst sort of manners to fight with your companion in another person's house. The thing to do when you have an argument brewing is to go get away from everybody before you have it out. Linda's accident with the heater corner didn't cause any serious injury, but it taught her a lesson about popping off like that.

In another instance, a young man was acting macho with his car one Saturday evening. "Davey" whipped it into a nightclub parking lot. The twenty-year-old car hit a bump in the pavement at such a high speed that it knocked something loose in the chassis.

The 1956 Chevrolet station wagon sputtered to a halt, and you could hear something on the underside of the car scraping along the pavement. Davey looked under it, went into the bar and got a mechanically-inclined friend to help him out. The damage was so bad they'd have to call a certified mechanic, and in those pre-AAA days there was none to be found at that time of night.

Davey and his friend pushed the car into a lot across the street, and Davey pitched the biggest public temper tantrum you ever heard in your life. He beat on the hood, the top and the windows as he screamed curses at the top of his lungs, and at one point got out a tire tool and beat on the car with that, until he broke the front window. This commotion got the crowd out of the nightclub, and about 20 people stood around gawking at this bit of street theater. Some people were laughing at it. Everybody knew what caused it and nobody bothered to help him. The nightclub didn't have live entertainment, but Davey sure provided some that night.

This happened more than 30 years ago, but the people who witnessed it still laugh about it.

Confucius had a saying, "If you plot revenge, you must first dig two graves." A friend of mine heard pharmacist Joe Graedon say that on a segment of the National Public Radio program "The People's Pharmacy." This show dealt with the ill effects of long-term resentment.

Unfortunately, "Chandler" had an unresolved issue of his own. He had lost a job several years ago, and although he later found another job and even liked it better, he still stewed sometimes over the way his old boss treated him.

Around the anniversary of his departure from that company, Chandler went out for a jog early one weekend morning. He was about a block from his old plant when he finished jogging. At that moment, he felt a call of nature and decided to answer it in the company's parking lot. There was nobody working in the plant at the time, and so he figured it wouldn't be doing that much harm.

As he walked to the plant, Chandler changed his mind about this particular act, but he had to go so badly that the lot was the only secluded place he could go. He started across an adjacent parking lot to carry out what he had originally planned. This adjacent lot was being re-surfaced—and it had a portable toilet for the work crew.

Chandler dashed into it and did his stuff, sparing his old employer's property, without carrying out an act of vengeance that he would have certainly felt silly about later.

"I don't believe that happened," Chandler said. "It's like, Somebody Up There put that portable toilet in my path, like it was a way of telling me to back off and put it behind me."

"I hated that boss for years. I kept my mouth shut at the time he was letting me go, knowing he was pre-pared to call the police if I lost it. I wanted so badly to go in there and chew him to the bone after that," he added.

"It's been a week since that time I stopped myself from doing my business in the plant parking lot—or I think more accurately, Somebody Up There stopped me," Chandler said. "But you know what? I don't have the anger spells I used to have after I got fired. I'm not going to go over there and say, 'Let's be buddies again,' but I've just quit stewing over it and having all these fantasies of throwing Molotov cocktails and siccing rabid Rottweilers on the manager. Thoughts like that have just stopped burrowing into my head."

I had planned to include among these anecdotes an encounter between a friend of mine and his rather vindic-tive neighbor, in which the neighbor got his come-up-pance. Before I started this piece, however, my friend "Ross" asked me not to put down the details, and so I'm respecting his wishes.

"I don't want him thinking he can still push my buttons," Ross said. "I have bigger things to deal with than this dumb feud. The difference between him and a gnat buzzing around your head is—you can't use an insect repellent on his species. It'd be nice if you could. End of subject, man."

One last little tale: Writing this tale brought back a childhood memory.

When I was 12 or 13 I used to catch bees and fireflies inside jars, poking holes in the lids so they could breathe. I let them go after awhile and even put things in the jars that I thought they could eat.

One bumblebee I caught didn't exactly appreciate my hospitality, so he (she?) started buzzing up a storm. It was a hot July day and my parents and I were sitting around in the dining room. The jar with the bumblebee sat on one of the cabinets, with the unwitting tenant carrying on. Well, after awhile, that buzzing got on my father's nerves so badly, he cried out, "Oh, for Chrissakes!"

Suddenly the room fell silent. The bumblebee had shut up at the exact moment of Dad's outburst.

Mom and I almost fell on the floor with laughter. It was as if this five-foot-seven ogre had scared the wits out of my little friend. At that moment Mom and I gave the bumblebee a name: "Little Chrissakes." Then I went outside with the jar and set Little Chrissakes free.

a
novella

The Bait

The pilot gritted his teeth. He drummed his fingers on the panel of the Gobbod Security Force landcar. The car hovered in an alley across from the Red Raptor Inn.

The pilot and his older partner watched the inhabitants of the planet Embricon and the Gobbod soldiers. The oil on their faces gleamed under the streetlights.

The gray-uniformed occupation troops and their fellow Gobbods in the Imperial Aerospace Fleet let the heels of their hands rest on their shouldered Jooblers. The inhabitants glowered at them.

"Strof, they're here," the young pilot said. He pointed to a Terramagnan couple striding up the sidewalk.

The older man cleared his throat. The pilot gulped. "I mean, Constable Strof."

The poker-faced Strof put a wireless to his mouth. He spoke into it as he watched the two Terramagnans.

Janniver Vrek and her older brother headed to the Red Raptor Inn. Three soldiers from a Gobbod troop-transport battalion came the other way. One of them bumped into Janniver before she could step out of his way.

"Ooh, pardon me, sweet thing," the Gobbod said, smirking.

The soldiers tipped their kepis to the two Terramagnans and walked on. They snickered as they slapped each other on the back.

One of them reached for his Joobler. He jerked his shoulder forward as if he were going to draw the weapon.

That set off another round of laughter from the three slimy-faced Gobbods.

Janniver shook her fist at them. Miklan moved in front of her. He nudged his sister away from the Gobbods. "Keep your cool, kid. Keep your cool," he said.

Janniver saw the Gobbod Security Force landcar across the street from the inn.

"Stinking Gobs are watching us everywhere we go," she said.

"Don't stare at them," Miklan said. "And quit being so jumpy. Alpha One's looking out for us."

"Really? Where is he?"

"Closer than you think." Miklan winked at her. "Believe me."

The streets of downtown Lofpuril swelled with people as the dull orange sun settled on the skyline. Although the Gobbod occupation government had imposed a law forbidding Embricon inhabitants to drink alcohol, many of the Embricons still went to the nightclubs and taverns. The Terramagnans and the Morkon Islanders could only purchase food and non-alcoholic drinks. They continued to go to the pubs and nightclubs for patriotic reasons, to keep them in business with Terramagnan money.

A group of Embricons, including two men from the Morkon Islands, stepped around the Vreks and went into the Red Raptor Inn. Miklan glanced at the Gobbod car in the alley. He raised his arm and quickly brought it down. Then he steered Janniver into the inn.

Bregna Keldon, the fifty-year-old proprietor, poured two goblets of pyongo juice.

"Welcome, welcome, my friends."

"Ist da mai-yor yet arrifed?" Janniver spoke with the accent of one of the languages of the planet Prax.

She had majored in intergalactic studies at the university.

"No, bubareeka, da ist not yet arrifed," Miklan said. He grinned. "But yet arrifed will he be, and da sooner we dissort him, da sooner you can stop the talking like dis."

Janniver punched him on the shoulder. "Oh, cut it out—I mean, halt da sport. Me you befuddle."

Bregna leaned across the bar. "Don't get her tickled, Vrek."

Janniver looked around. She moved around the bar, next to Bregna. "Ah, excuse me, Mrs. Keldon, have you heard anything about Lieutenant Krin?"

Bregna took her by the arm. She led her into the stockroom. "I told you, we cannot discuss Avralian activities."

"I know, but I just can't stand not knowing about him," Janniver said.

She clutched the silver medallion beneath her tunic. Drakko Krin had given it to her before he entered flight school.

"My dear, I feel for you," Bregna said. "But the less we know about allied movements, the better for them. And the better for Firewave. Do not ask again."

Then she smiled. "But I can tell you, child, your man is mighty hard to kill."

A server led a couple from the Morkon Islands and three Terramagnans to a corner booth. For Gobbod sappers in dull brown uniforms sat three stalls away.

His eye on the Gobbods, Miklan took a small silvery-blue disk from his tunic. He held it under the bar and touched it to his thigh. In ten seconds the metallic disk changed to the same deep shade of green as his trousers.

"What is that?" Janniver said. "Okh, I remember."

Miklan tucked the jamming disk back into his tunic.

He had shown it to Janniver during the final briefing with Alpha One's head of Mission Command. "You get enough of these little fiends and it's goodbye, Gobbies."

Bregna tapped Miklan on the arm. Janniver looked behind her.

Five gray-clad Gobbods with shaven heads came into the tavern. One pumped his fist in the air twice.

"Don't turn around," Bregna whispered. "They're ground troops, not Krentox."

The Gobbod soldiers passed by the sappers' booth. One of the sappers thrust three fingers at the soldiers, making an obscene gesture. Two soldiers slapped their upper arms at the sappers. Both groups of Gobbods broke into laughter.

Janniver balled her fists. She clenched her teeth and rolled her eyes upward.

Miklan sipped his pyongo juice. He squeezed his eyes shut and twisted his mouth into a wry frown. "I also hate it," Bregna said.

Bregna and her husband had opened the Red Raptor years before the Gobbod conquest. They closed it when they joined the Terramagnan army. Bregna's husband Johevy had one of his hands blown off by a grenade in the fighting. After the surrender, the Gobbods forced Bregna to re-open the Red Raptor. Now Bregna managed the inn, while her Johevy looked after the house and fed their three cats.

A hover cruiser with the jagged cross and hawk wings of the Imperial Gobbod Aerospace Fleet stopped outside the inn. Two slimy-cheeked officers in scarlet dress jackets stepped out as the vehicle hovered above the pavement.

Bregna peered into the stockroom. "Now," she said.

The Gobbod hovercruiser glided around the corner, onto the parking deck. The two Hawkship pilots stood outside the inn until a tall, broad-shouldered officer approached them.

The three men walked in. Besides the usual fighter pilot's insignia, the broad-shouldered officer wore major's crosses on his epaulets. Four silver and gold medals gleamed on his left breast. He also wore small crescent-shaped pins on both his sleeves, twenty-seven in all. Each one stood for an Avralian vessel he claimed to have destroyed.

He puffed out his chest. The other oily-skinned Gobbods pointed to him.

Miklan tapped Janniver on the shoulder. "Act One, Scene One," he whispered.

Janniver swiveled around on her bar stool and slapped Miklan across the face.

"Keep your hands to the self, you," she said. Miklan rubbed his reddening cheek. "You little tart," he said. He took a napkin and spat blood on it.

Janniver gasped. "I didn't mean to hit him that hard," she whispered to Bregna.

Bregna put her finger to her closed lips, then turned to Miklan. "You have insulted my patrons for the last time, you swine. Get out now and don't come back."

Miklan snatched his jacket and headed for the gate. He shook his finger at Bregna. "You're in for it now, you old hag." He ran outside.

The Gobbod major and his two friends strode to the bar. "Is there a problem here, bird?" the major asked.

"No. Nothing. Am all right, sir," Janniver said.

"What did that Terrod say to you?" the major asked. He turned to Bregna. "Did you serve him any spirits, madame publady?"

Something cold shot up Janniver's spine, like an electric sword. She shivered.

She remembered her Praxi accent. "No. She no serve him," she said. "He-he drink before to come here. Madame Keldon no serve him. Is why he thus dissorted."

The gap-toothed Gobbod jerked his thumb at the door. "Our security troopers will deal with that fool," he said. "Hm. Let me you ask something, bird. Who escorted you within here?"

"I wait my friend girl. She late," Janniver said.

"Just you two?" the gap-toothed Gobbod said. "No masculine escort?"

"No. My friend, myself only and alone," Janniver said.

The third Gobbod rubbed his chin. He had a purplish-red boil on his cheek. It looked like a small ripe plum. "That fellow causing you trouble, you know, I saw him before," he said.

"He looks like that Terrod who won the University games ten-thousand-meter run a couple of years ago," the gap-toothed Gobbod said. "You remember him, do you not, Major Krentox? What was his name? Vrek?"

Krentox shook his head. "No. That could not be him. Why would someone so famous be lurking about in this bombed-out place? If he survived the invasion, he's hiding out in an Avralian refugee camp."

He turned to Janniver. "Do you really not know who that man was?"

Janniver threw up her arms. "I tell truth. Never see him until I come here."

The gap-toothed Gobbod picked at his crotch. "Speaking of foreign athletes, Major, do you also remember that Avroid sprinter from the University of Green-moon Nine?" he said. "Drakko Krin?"

74

Janniver tried not to stare at him.

A wet belch gurgled out of his mouth. "I heard reports that we've just captured him."

The blood rushed to Janniver's face. Her head felt hot. She felt as if she were going to explode.

She wanted to jump on top of the enemy pilot and tear out his throat. If she had a knife or a blaster she would have killed them all, those puffy-chested slobs strutting about in her streets, her country, her homeworld.

The gap-toothed Gobbod backhanded the pilot with the boil, squarely in his chest.

"Listen to this, Nopkosh," he said. "This Krin tschong's a Daggerwing pilot. A friend of mine in security's brother has a friend in the Fifty-Fifth Predators."

The major and the pilot with the boil stared at him.

"Last month they wiped out a squadron of Avroids around the Menzenian Moons," the gap-toothed Gobbod said. "Five-Five blew up nine of the Daggerwings, but they took three pilot's prisoner. My friend's brother heard that Krin tschong was one of them."

"You're joking," said the pilot with the plum boil. "The Drakko Krin, a prisoner of the Empire?"

"I'm as serious as the yellow crungs, Nopkosh," the gap-toothed Gobbod said.

Oh, dear God, Janniver thought.

She realized she was falling. She caught herself against a chair before she hit the floor. Without thinking, she grabbed Drakko's medallion beneath her tunic.

"What's wrong with you, bird?" the gap-toothed Gobbod said. "You look as if one just clopped you on the head."

Janniver let go of the hidden medallion. "I-I think I eat bad food. Excuse me. I be sick."

She headed to the entrance. "The lavatory's upstairs," Frak Krentox said.

"Ak, yes. I forget."

Janniver spun around and stumbled to the stairs. The chain from Drakko's medallion cut into the back of her neck. She covered her mouth as she climbed the stairs.

Bregna followed her into the lavatory. Janniver splashed cold water on her face.

Bregna pushed the door to. "What's the matter, Vrek?" the publady asked.

"Did you know about Drakko? Did you?"

"No time to discuss this now," Bregna said.

"They got him." Janniver almost screamed it. "Those fremkopi were bragging about it down there. And you knew, didn't you?"

She blurted out what the gap-toothed Gobbod said. "I can't believe you'd keep that from me."

"Now listen to me," Bregna said. "There was nothing to keep from anybody. That story's false."

"False?"

"Alpha One didn't want you to hear it," Bregna said. "It's a lie we've been feeding to Gobbod intelligence."

"What do you mean?"

Bregna clasped the younger woman by the hair. "All right. The second I tell you this I want you to forget it," Bregna whispered.

"We have some agents in their security force," Bregna said after a moment. "One of the pilots goes to their headquarters all the time, and one of our plants sort of made friends with him. He told the pilots this story about Lieutenant Krin to test his gullibility, to test the efficiency of their intelligence units."

"But, why?" Janniver said. "Why tell him something

like that?"

Bregna sighed. "Orders from Alpha One," she said. "I don't know his reasons. But I assure you, Lieutenant Krin is very much alive."

Janniver shook her head. "What kind of person is this Alpha One?"

Two Terramagnan females came in. "What's with her?" one of them asked.

"Too much flurkfish," Bregna said.

She led Janniver out. They sat on a bench outside the lavatory. "I'm sorry I went off like that," Janniver said.

"Go back down there and let Frak Krentox chat you up," Bregna said. "Now. He's not going to stay here all evening."

Janniver turned to her. "Mrs. Keldon, I'm glad that wasn't true about Drakko, but I'm still so upset I could tear that Gob's gonads off with my bare hands. I mean it. Can't Alpha One let me do something else?"

Bregna took Janniver by both arms. "Absolutely not. Alpha One will expel you from Firewave if you quit this mission. He'll ship you to Prax and keep you there under guard until we drive out the Gobbods. Do you understand?"

Janniver nodded. She wiped her nose.

"And don't even think about walking out of this pub," Bregna said. "You won't get ten meters out the door before our other agents will pick you up. Clear?"

"Oh, no," Janniver said. "Do you really think I'd do that?"

"You need to prove to Alpha One that you wouldn't," Bregna said.

She tugged Janniver to her feet. "Come, don't keep your guests waiting."

Frak Krentox stood at the landing. "Are you all

right?" he asked Janniver.

Janniver nodded. "Better now. Thank you."
Nopkosh, the pilot with the boil, said, "Don't you worry,
little bird. We'll sort out that Terrod turf jockey if he's
stupid enough to come back."

"We certainly hope this bird's right about you not
serving him," the gap-toothed Gobbod said to Bregna.
"You have a nice place here. We'd hate to close it down
because you by serving spirits to the natives have violated
Imperial law. We don't want any more to lock up a single
pubkeeper," he added. "Even if they are Terrod
monkeys."

"Let her be, Greepog," Nopkosh said. "She's the
only native who doesn't spit in the drinks."

Frak Krentox turned to Janniver. "You are not
Terramagnan, are you?" he said. "I assure you, my fellow
officers will for their remarks apologize, will you not, my
brothers in arms?"

Janniver looked at the floor. She bit her index fin-
ger as her face turned red. "That is no matter, officer-
pilot. I come from Prax."

Krentox cocked his head. "Ah, Prax. What a de-
lightful planet. I could drink the stout on your homeworld
by the drum."

He held up his hand. "Not that I actually consume
such quantities at one time," he said. "But I spent on your
homeworld a single year. I was an exchange student at the
Free University before the war. But tell me, tender one,
what are you doing on Embricon?"

"I-I am on semester leave. From the Free Univers-
ity." Janniver could not remember the other schools on
Prax.

Krentox touched his chin. "Coming to Embricon
to spend your leave?" he said. "The Empire of Gobbod

has this planet completely under martial law. As you must have learned, the Avralians are trying to invade Embricon. This is not a safe place, tender one."

From the corner of her eye, Janniver caught Bregna's pained expression.

"Oh, I-I come to stop by my uncle," Janniver said.

"Did you?" Krentox said. "And how does your uncle make a living now on Embricon?"

"He, ah, he operates a—a how you say?—an inter-planetary exporting business."

"Still? Even after Embricon lost the war," Krentox said. "What does he export?"

Janniver's throat felt dry. "Pyongo fruit."

Krentox leaned against the bar and let out a laugh. "Pyongos," he said.

"Two years ago, His Excellency's troops all but pounded this world into ashes. And yet has this fellow remained behind that he could continue to sell tropical citrus fruit," Krentox said. "I would like really like to shake his hand, this entrepreneur uncle you claim exists."

Janniver glanced at Bregna. The publady pointed outside. "He, ah, he exports the pyongo fruit to Prax," Janniver said. "He-he deal only with-with peoples who hate Avralians."

Krentox grinned, then shrugged his shoulders. "Ah, well. It is good to met someone from a neutral system. I tell you, you really must come to Gobbod. Especially the Imperial City. Operas, art museums, jontee tournaments, parks, really a beautiful place."

He slapped the holster of his Joobler. Then he raised his arm and whistled.

"Madame publady. Serve our Praxi friend whatever she pleases."

Bregna leaned over the bar.

"I think I shall have Golden Island lager," Janniver said.

"The same for myself, Madame publady," Krentox said.

Half an hour later, Janniver and Frak Krentox were sitting in a Gobbod landcar, in the parking deck. She let the Gobbod kiss her and put his arms around her.

I never imagined doing things like this for the motherworld, Janniver thought.

Stop it, stop it, stop it, she told herself. This is vile. Nothing funny about it all. This creature and his friends killed your people. He and his friends are all laughing because they think they just put the man you love in a cage.

Janniver tried to imagine it was Drakko in the hovercruiser with her, it was Drakko who had his arms and mouth all over her, not this—this slob—who reeked of cheap face oil and looked like a spiky-haired dog on a parade float.

The Gobbod's oily skin gleamed in the streetlight. Drakko had healthy, sweet-smelling skin. Not like these Gobs. How can their women stand them?

Janniver tried not to gag as she kissed Frak Krentox down the side of his face.

Janniver remembered holding one of the zogcarp her father had caught when she was six. The oil on Krentox's cheeks reminded her of the slimy coat on the fish's body.

Laughter bubbled up in Janniver's chest. She took a deep breath, but she couldn't stop a snort of laughter from exploding from her mouth and spraying Krentox all over his face.

"What's the matter with you? Spitting all over me?"

"Oh, oh, no, I so sorry, I choke on something,"

Janniver said. "Please pardon, no?"

Krentox shook his head. "I've never met a bird like you, Praxi."

The landcar gave off a faint buzzing sound.

A purple light flashed on and off on the pilot's side of the console.

"Why you power engine?" Janniver asked.

"Let me show you something," Krentox said.

He punched three buttons. The landcar began to move.

"A forcebelt automatically straps you in while the cruiser's in motion," he said.

He turned to the Terramagnan and grinned. "Great way to restrain enemy captives, don't you think?"

"Ah, ah, yes."

Krentox changed his grin to a stern, slit-eyed look. He uncovered another panel of controls. "Plus, it works excellently on Embricon subversives masquerading as neutral offworlders."

Janniver's heart sank. "Ex-excuse?"

"You are not a Praxi," Krentox said. "Tell me the truth. Where do you come from?"

"I am from Prax. Why say you that?"

The landcar turned left. It floated past the inn and started up the street. "I could turn you in to security," Krentox said. "But you are much too pretty to send to a prison camp. Oh, yes, we have constructed a very hot compound on this planet. So I think we'll go out on the open path."

"Open path?"

Krentox took her hand. "I'll let you try to convince me not to bring you in for interrogation."

"You bastard," Janniver said. She groped inside the door for a handle.

"No use trying to escape, little fly," the Gobbod said. "But don't be so frightened. I'm not going to do anything you might have seen in this awful Avroid propaganda disks."

He stroked the trembling Terramagnan's angel-fine hair. His tongue snaked out of his leering mouth. "Why don't you just settle back and enjoy the ride," the Gobbod whispered. "Let me show you what this splendid work of Imperial craftsmanship can do."

The engine stopped.

The compartment went dark as the lights on the controls faded.

The hovercruiser struck the ground. It bounced twice with a screech like a scalded giant, then crashed into a light pole, throwing Janniver and Krentox out of their deactivated harnesses. Janniver grabbed the top of her seat before her head struck the front panel.

The Terramagnan woman threw all her weight against the passenger door. Krentox was groaning and holding his head. The door did not budge. Janniver dug her fingers into the edge of the door and pulled as hard as she could. It moved a foot.

Something small hit the window and exploded six inches from Janniver's head.

Krentox was pointing his Joobler at her.

"Make another move and I'll aim for your ear."

"Don't kill me. Please." Janniver's voice came out in a dry squeak.

"You had your chance, you Terrod whore," Krentox said. "You and your little friends run around in the shadows, calling yourselves freedom fighters. But you're all just a bunch of cowards and hoodlums. Hiding out in cellars like rats."

"I-I don't—I don't know wh-wh-what you're

talking about."

Krentox fired again. Something hot zipped over the right side of Janniver's abdomen. She glanced down. The slug had singed a six-inch slit in her tunic, but she did not see any blood.

"Lucky again, Terrod," Krentox said. "What an act, you with that accent and your pyongo-seller uncle. Your turdbag friends must be so desperate they'll take anybody stupid enough to believe their nonsense."

He aimed the Joobler at Janniver's left eye.

"I hoped you would not force me to do this. But you leave me no choice. You're about to find out what the Gobbod Empire does to cowards, common killers and skulky little tramps like you."

The Gobbod reached between Janniver's breasts. His fingers closed around Drakko's medallion beneath her tunic.

"Oh, ho, what's this, then?" Krentox said. "Maybe a little souvenir for your friendly Gobbod liberators? Let's have a look."

He pulled her towards him.

The door slid open.

Janniver swung her forearm upward and knocked the Gobbod's hand from her chest. The sides of her tunic ripped open. She tumbled over backwards, but somebody caught her before she hit the ground.

"We've got her, Major," the pilot from the security force landcar said.

Constable Strof turned Janniver right side up. He helped her to her feet. "Who are you?" she asked.

"Constable Strof and Private Arnk of the Gobbod Security Force, my lady," the older officer said.

"That woman's mine, Constable," Krentox said.

"The fleet will deal with her."

"With all due respect, sir, this is security's jurisdiction," Strof said.

Arnk, the pilot, tied Janniver's wrists together. She looked at the ground as he led her to the security landcar.

"You'd better make her talk," Krentox called out. The security hovercruiser idled beside the wrecked car. Arnk slid the door open. He pushed Janniver into the front seat and climbed in after her. Constable Strof walked toward Krentox and started talking to him.

Janniver's chin trembled. "Officer, I—why are you arresting me?"

"For membership in the Firewave," Arnk said.

"But I don't know what you're talking about."

The pilot grinned. "Oh, yes, you do."

Janniver heard three dull thumping sounds. One of the men groaned. Someone crashed against the wrecked landcar and fell to the ground.

The door slid shut. Arnk punched a button. An invisible forcebelt bound Janniver in the seat.

"We don't want you running away before we show you something," Arnk said.

He got out. Strof had his arm around Frak Krentox. The fighter pilot was unconscious, his hands shackled behind his back.

Arnk helped Strof roll him into the back seat. "Oh, no, is he dead?" Janniver said.

She started breathing hard. "I-I—I didn't mean to kill him. I swear it. He had too much to drink and he was . . . ."

"Oh, pipe down. He'll be fine," Strof said. He clambered into the back seat, beside the unconscious Krentox.

"At least until he spends a few months in one of our cells," Strof said.

84

"You mean you're arresting him, too?" Janniver said. "What for?"

Strof broke into laughter. "I don't believe it," he said.

He turned to the pilot. "Omega Seven, we make such good Gobbod police our own people don't even recognize us."

Arnk reached down and unlocked Janniver's shackles.

"You can stop freaking out now," the pilot said. "We're in Firewave, too. Janniver Vrek, meet our honorable commander-in-chief."

He nodded to Strof. "Alpha One."

"That's right," Strof said. "We are all Firewave."

"You mean . . ."

"Agent Omega Seven and I have been staking out the inn all evening, keeping an eye on you and your brother," Strof said.

"While you were keeping our friend here—ah— occupied, your brother sneaked out to the parking deck and planted one of his scrambledisks onto the undercarriage. That's how he crippled that landcar."

"Oh, my God," Janniver said. "I don't believe it. But what about Lieutenant Krin? The Gobbods haven't really taken him prisoner, have they?"

Alpha One's smile disappeared. His mouth grew taut and his eyebrows leveled off. "I thought Bregna told you he was still with his unit," he barked. "You telling me you don't believe her?"

Janniver gulped. "Beg your pardon, sir. I shall not ask again."

Alpha One turned to the pilot. "Well, what are you waiting for? Let's get out of here."

"Sir, yes sir." Omega Seven put the car in motion.

"But, sir, ah, Alpha One," Janniver said. "How did you get this car? Those uniforms?"

"Ssh," Alpha One said.

The poker-faced older man looked at Frak Krentox. The big Gobbod moved his head and groaned.

Alpha One looked away.

"I don't have the heart to tell him how easily we infiltrated their efficient security force and commandeered one of their vehicles," he said. "A damn sight easier than keeping tabs on you and your brother, my dear."

Agent Omega Seven put his hand over his mouth. Janniver sighed. "I shall do better next time, Alpha One," she said. "Granted that I am allowed to remain in Firewave."

Alpha One snorted. He waved his arm at her. "Oh, don't be so mousy. Both of you played your parts tremendously well. We have been trying to capture this Fremkop for months and you and your brother did it."

He turned to Krentox. "Better make yourself at home, my friend," he said. "You're going to be here for a long, long time."

finis

acknowledgments

We've often heard it said, "It takes a village to raise a child." The same applies to publishing a book.

I wish to thank a whole team of people for supporting me with the invaluable gift of their time while I seriously considered becoming an author. I'm very grateful for their presence in my life.

My thanks to my closest friends for urging me to get a book published after seeing my various poems, essays, fiction, song lyrics and other writings over the years. Among these friends are Morrie Hitson, Barbara Rich, William Schloegl, Debra Reece Simons and Mary Dorner Stephens.

I'd like to celebrate my newest friend—my publisher, Karen Mireau. As founder of Azalea Art Press, her expertise and artistic skills helped me design a book that we hope everyone will enjoy.

Admiration must be expressed for my former high school language arts instructor, Brenda Phelps, for the many things I learned from her in both dramatics and literature. Thanks also to another former English instructor, the late Sue Owen, for once telling me I'd be a fool not to keep on writing.

Greg McNair deserves a very special mention for his friendship, his guidance during my first full-time job in journalism, and for his awesome preface to this book.

Former Daily Journal publisher Neal Cadieu and his daughter Beth, now an accomplished high-school journalism instructor, have been great supporters in years past as well as valued friends, as have Helen Cox and her husband, the late Clark Cox. Thanks to them all.

My deepest gratitude goes to the late William Edwin and Elizabeth Sanders Lindau, my parents; and my older sister, Sara Lindau, for being such a splendid family —all of them writers.

about
the author

      Bill Lindau, known to his friends as "Wild Bill," was born in Asheville, North Carolina and lived in Winston-Salem before moving to Southern Pines at age fourteen. He attended East Carolina University and Sandhills Community College before earning a B.A. in Comparative Literature from the University of North Carolina at Chapel Hill.

Bill has written for newspapers in various capacities since 1983 and contributed book reviews to local newspapers before then. He has spent most of his life in the North Carolina Sandhills since his teens, but has also lived in Chapel Hill and Richmond County. He has traveled in Europe and worked in a pub in Nottingham, England in a work-exchange program with the United Kingdom.

Bill also dabbles in art and participates in community theater. He performs Americana and contemporary love ballads at local open mic nights, singing and playing the digital keyboard, with some original songs included. He now resides in Southern Pines with his two cats.

The author welcomes your comments
and correspondence. You can reach
Bill Lindau at:

blindau52@yahoo.com
910-331-7477
https://www.facebook.com/billwlindau/
www.linkedin.com/pub/bill-lindau/36/682/477

A Special Thank You—
Cover Photographer
John Roger Palmour

John Roger Palmour is a completely self taught, amateur photographer and keen gardener who lives in Georgia with Marty, his wife of over 40 years.

His prize-winning images have appeared in *Horticulture Magazine* as well as in the International Garden Photographer of the Year Contest sponsored by the Royal Botanical Gardens at Kew in London. Most recently, one of his photographs won the Nature's Pharmacy Award and was displayed at the New York Botanical Garden.

This evocative photograph titled "Sunrise in the Longleaf Pine Forest" captures the magic that Roger and his wife saw in that brief moment when the sun first pops through the morning haze.

We are very grateful to Roger and Marty for their creative vision and for Roger's generosity in allowing us to adapt this award-winning photo for the cover of this book. You can view Roger's photo gallery online at http://www.flickr.com/photos/ugardener.

Azalea Art Press
specializes in giving personal attention
to authors who wish to realize
their literary and creative dreams.

To learn more about writing,
designing and successfully marketing
your next print, e-reader or e-book,
please get in touch with:

Karen Mireau
Azalea.Art.Press@gmail.com
azaleaartpress.blogspot.com

510.919.6117

To schedule an interview or signing
with the author, please contact the publisher.
This anthology by Bill Lindau
may be ordered directly at
www.lulu.com.

94

www.ingramcontent.com/pod-product-compliance
Lightning Source LLC
Chambersburg PA
CBHW020729250626

47155CB00006B/2221